TEN WHO
ROCKED
THE WORLD

Julius Lester
Illustrated by Lisa Cohen

JUMP AT THE SUN
HYPERION BOOKS FOR CHILDREN
NEW YORK

For my granddaughter, Page Samantha Lester.
—J. L.

For my daughter, Mischa ("This little light of mine"),
my husband, Sebastien, and my family near and far.
We join in celebrating the birth of Jackson Oliver Cohen.
—L. C.

Text © 2001 by Julius Lester
Illustrations © 2001 by Lisa Cohen

Visit www.jumpatthesun.com

Printed in Singapore
First Edition
1 3 5 7 9 10 8 6 4 2
This book is set in GoudySans Light.
Library of Congress Cataloging-in-Publication Data
Lester, Julius.
The blues singers : ten who rocked the world / Julius Lester ; illustrated by Lisa Cohen.—1st ed.
    p.   cm.
Includes bibliographical references (p.   ) and discography (p.   ).
ISBN 0-7868-0463-7 (trade)—ISBN 0-7868-2405-0 (lib. bdg.)
1. Blues musicians—United States—Biography—Juvenile literature. [1. Blues (Music) 2. Singers.
3. Afro-Americans—Biography.] I. Cohen, Lisa, 1963- ill. II. Title.
ML3929.L47 2001
781.643'092'2—dc21
[B]
00-59019

CONTENTS

A grandfather talks to his granddaughter

I sure am glad you came to visit again this summer. It makes me happy that you like to hear your grandfather's stories about different people in history. Last summer I told you stories about people like Frederick Douglass, W.E.B. Du Bois, and Martin Luther King, Jr. This summer I want to tell you about some of the great blues singers. I used to play the guitar and do a little singing, you know, and I saw a lot of blues singers. My father—that would be your *great*-grandfather—saw others.

That music you hear in the background is the blues. Many singers today are walking in the footsteps of blues singers like Bessie Smith, Blind Lemon Jefferson, Son House, Robert Johnson, and Muddy Waters, to name just a few.

Who're they? Well, I'm glad you asked. That's why there are grandfathers and grandmothers in the world. One of our jobs is to remember how things used to be so we can tell our grandchildren. My grandfather remembered Bessie and told me about her. I remembered Bessie from him, and Muddy Waters for myself, and I'm going to pass them on to you.

So what are the blues? Well, the blues are like having the flu in your feelings. But instead of your nose being stuffed up, it's your heart that feels like it needs blowing. Everybody gets the blues, even children.

But the blues is not only a feeling. It's also a kind of music that cures the blues. The words of a blues song might be sad, but the music and the beat wrap around your heart like one of your grandmother's hugs.

The roots of the blues go back to slavery. If anything would give you the blues, it was slavery. Imagine somebody owning you like I own my car. Just like I can sell my car to anybody who has the money, somebody could sell you and me the same way.

One of the ways black people fought against slavery was with the breath in their bodies. They wove hope on the air by singing songs called spirituals—songs for the spirit. Their bodies were in slavery, but it didn't mean their spirits had to be buried in sorrow as white as fog.

Slavery ended in 1865, but freedom didn't take its place. The people who had owned the slaves still owned the land. How could the slaves truly be free if they had to keep working for the same people who had owned them?

Blues music probably started something like this: Somebody was out in the field working one day. She knew she would be working from sunup to sundown on somebody's farm making fifty cents a day until the day she died. Thinking about it made her heart burn as if it had been struck by lightning. The pain was so bad she didn't know what to do, and suddenly she started singing:

> *Got a hurtin' in my heart, feels like I'm going to die,*
> *Got a hurtin' in my heart, feels like I'm going to die,*
> *I feel like a bird whose wings will never fly.*

Singing just those few words made her feel a little better, and everybody who heard her felt a little better, too.

So I'm going to tell you about ten blues singers who rocked the world. The United States government understood how important some of these singers were and put pictures of Bessie Smith, Muddy Waters, Billie Holiday, Robert Johnson, and Mahalia Jackson on postage stamps.

Honey, if it wasn't for the blues, we probably wouldn't have anything to listen to except our toenails growing. ▲

BESSIE SMITH

*Born April 15, 1894,
Chattanooga, Tennessee
Died September 26, 1937,
Clarksdale, Mississippi*

**Bessie was my favorite.
Her music haunted you
even when she stopped singing. / MAHALIA JACKSON**

The Empress of the Blues. That's what everybody called her. She was a big woman with a voice as wide and long as the sky.

Bessie Smith's father was a preacher, who died soon after she was born. By the time she was eight, her mother and a brother had died, leaving Bessie, her three sisters, and two brothers to make it the best way they could. Bessie made money by singing on street corners, with her brother, Andrew, playing guitar for her.

When she was around seventeen, she joined the Moses Stokes Traveling Show, where she met Ma Rainey, a singer who was called the Queen of the Blues. What is a traveling show? Well, back in the early 1900s there was no radio or television. But that didn't mean people sat in their houses and watched the darkness grow whiskers when the sun went down. A traveling show had a band, dancers, singers, and comedians. My grandfather said that when the traveling show came, they paraded through the streets to let folks know they were in town, then pitched their tent in a field and put on shows for a week or so. Bessie traveled around the South for eight years with various shows like that until she started her own.

In 1920, a woman named Mamie Smith, no kin to Bessie, put out the first blues record, called "Crazy Blues." (Records are what folks listened to before

CDs.) Three years later, Bessie made her first record, called "Downhearted Blues." It sold 780,000 copies, which would be a lot of records even today. Over the next seven years, Bessie recorded 160 songs and became the most famous blues singer, man or woman, of her time.

Bessie was so successful that she bought a yellow railroad car to carry her show in. It was seventy-eight feet long and her name was painted on the side in green lettering. It had seven staterooms, each one big enough for four people to sleep in. Thirty-five more slept on the lower level. That way the crew and all forty or so musicians, dancers, and comedians could travel together. There was still room in the railroad car for the tent and the cases of peanuts, Cracker Jacks, and sodas sold at her shows.

Because we can hear Bessie only on records, we think of her as a singer; but my grandfather said she acted in skits, told jokes, did pantomime, danced, *and* sang. She was a complete entertainer.

Bessie was also a woman you didn't want to mess with. She wasn't afraid of anybody, not even the Ku Klux Klan. One night in July 1927, Bessie was doing a show in a little place called Concord, North Carolina. It was hot in the tent, and one of Bessie's musicians went out to get some air. He heard strange voices and went to see what was going on. He came upon six members of the KKK, dressed in their white robes and wearing white pointed hoods over their heads, trying to pull out the stakes holding up Bessie's tent. If they did pull them out, the tent would fall in, and who knows how many people inside might be hurt or even killed.

The musician ran and told Bessie. The same spirit Bessie put into her singing, she put into her living. When she heard what the KKK was trying to do, Bessie cursed under her breath (something she did a lot anyway) and marched outside.

SHE WAS A BIG WOMAN WITH A VOICE AS WIDE AND LONG AS THE SKY

"What do you think you're doing?" she shouted at the Klansmen, putting one hand on her hip and shaking her fist at them. Bessie's language was a little stronger than that, but you get the idea. "You better pick up your sheets and get out of here!"

And they did.

Bessie died in a car accident outside Clarksdale, Mississippi, in 1937, and she was buried near Philadelphia, Pennsylvania, where she had lived. Ten thousand people walked by her casket and thirty-nine cars were in the funeral procession. But as famous as she was, somehow her relatives forgot to put a headstone on her grave.

In 1970 a black woman named Barbara Muldow wrote to a Philadelphia newspaper, upset that Bessie Smith lay in an unmarked grave. Juanita Green, of the National Association for the Advancement of Colored People (NAACP), and Janis Joplin, the blues-rock singer many compared to Bessie, each gave half the money to buy a tombstone. Ironically, Janis Joplin died on October 4, 1970, two months after the tombstone was unveiled and on the same date as Bessie Smith's funeral thirty-three years before.

Bessie died two years before I was born. She was the Empress of the Blues then and she's the Empress of the Blues now. ▲

robert
johnson

johnson

*Born May 8, 1911,
Hazelhurst, Mississippi
Died August 16, 1938,
Greenwood, Mississippi*

**One time in
St. Louis he was
playing very slow
and passionately,
and when we had
quit, I noticed no
one was saying
anything. Then
I realized they
were crying—both
women and men.
JOHNNY SHINES,
BLUES SINGER**

**He'd get a feeling, and out
of nowhere he could put a song
together. I remember asking him
about songs he'd sung two or three nights
before, and he'd tell me he couldn't do that one
again. And I'd ask him why. He'd say, "Well, I was
just, just reciting from a feeling."
HENRY TOWNSEND, BLUES SINGER**

**If Bessie Smith is Empress of
the Blues, Robert Johnson is
King of the Delta Blues Singers.**
And if you're the king of the blues
singers who came out of the part
of Mississippi they call the Delta,
then you're king of *all* the blues
singers.

Your great-grandfather was
from Mississippi, and he said he
saw Robert a couple of times at a
jook joint on somebody's plantation. What's a jook joint? Well, it
was like a bar, except it was in
somebody's cabin where you
could buy moonshine whiskey and
dance to live music. Moonshine

The sound Robert Johnson got from his guitar was so unusual and eerie that people said nobody could play like that unless he had made a deal with

whiskey was illegal liquor made from corn. When I was recording blues singers in Mississippi and Alabama in the 1960s, I spent more than one night in jook joints listening to music and watching people dance.

One of the first things folks noticed about Robert Johnson was his long, slender fingers. The next thing was how neatly he dressed. Robert looked as if his suit, white shirt, and tie had gone directly from the ironing board to his body. It didn't matter if he was walking along a country road on a hot summer day, guitar in hand, or riding all night on a freight train. The creases in his pants stayed as sharp as a slave's longing for freedom. The dirt and dust seemed to have made a deal with him not to get on his clothes, and Brother Sun turned back his rays so Robert wouldn't sweat.

Nobody made music like Robert Johnson. The sound he got from his guitar was so unusual and eerie that people said nobody could play like that unless he had made a deal with ol' Satan. Robert played the guitar with a metal slide or the broken-off neck of a bottle on one of the fingers of his left hand. Sometimes it's hard to tell if it is him or the guitar singing, because they sound so much alike. He was a natural musician and could hear a song once on the radio and play it back exactly as he'd heard it.

Robert's voice was high, like a woman's, but not like any woman who walked the earth. But if the dead could sing, and if anyone dared listen, that's what Robert Johnson sounded like. His voice was like sorrow, as white as the bones of a man who was lynched and is looking for a place to sleep and knows he'll never find it.

There's nothing else I can tell you about Robert Johnson. Not much is known about his life, what little of it there was. He was only twenty-seven when he died. They say he was given a bottle of poisoned whiskey by the husband of a woman he was getting too friendly with. But others think ol' Satan came and said, "Time's up, Robert. I already got your soul. Now I want your body to go with it." ◢

ol' Satan

Mahalia JACKSON

Born October 26, 1911, New Orleans, Louisiana
Died January 27, 1972, Chicago, Illinois

When black people stop singing the blues, then there'll be no more nothin'!
Because the blues has made American music and they will still be around when
all the rock and stuff has gone. The blues is always around. / MAHALIA JACKSON

Mahalia Jackson!
Lord, she was a singing lady! / RAY CHARLES

Mahalia Jackson was not a blues singer. She sang church songs, gospel, but she knew blues and brought the blues feeling into church music. Other people, like Ray Charles and Aretha Franklin, grew up singing gospel, too, but they took the gospel feeling and put it into the blues. The words in a gospel song and the words in the blues will be different, but both can make you start moaning like you've just bitten into the best fried chicken anybody ever made. So that's why you have to know about Mahalia Jackson. Even if she didn't sing the blues, she learned a lot from listening to blues singers, and blues singers have learned a lot from listening to her sing gospel.

Mahalia grew up in New Orleans, Louisiana, the city where jazz was born and where there is still more good music and good food per block than anyplace in the world. Her father worked on the docks during the day loading bales of cotton on boats, was a barber at night and a preacher on Sundays. When Mahalia was five years old her mother died. Her father took her to live with Mahalia Paul, an aunt who lived nearby and the woman for whom Mahalia Jackson was named. Mahalia never lived with her father again, but she saw him almost every day at his barbershop.

Mahalia grew up loving music, and the person she wanted to sing like was none other than Bessie Smith. But Mahalia's aunt was very religious, and she took Mahalia to church every day. When talking about her childhood, Mahalia said that in her church, "everybody sang and clapped and stomped their feet, sang with their whole bodies! They had the beat, a powerful beat, a rhythm we held on to from slavery days, and [the] music was so strong and expressive, it used to bring the tears to my eyes." It was in church that Mahalia first started singing.

She dropped out of school after the eighth grade and went to work doing people's laundry. Mahalia began hearing stories from relatives and friends about how good life was in Chicago, Illinois. So when she was sixteen, another aunt, Hannah, took her to Chicago to live. Once there, Mahalia joined a gospel group and a church choir while working during the day as a maid in hotels.

It was in Chicago that Mahalia got the chance to see her idol, Bessie Smith, who came to town to put on a show. Years later Mahalia remembered that Bessie "filled the whole place with her voice [and] I never went home until they put us out and closed up for the night."

Mahalia's singing brought her to the attention of Thomas A. Dorsey, who directed a number of gospel choirs in Chicago. Dorsey was the father of gospel music, but earlier

Mahalia

could go from a high note to a low one as easily as you put one foot in front of the other

in his life he had been the pianist for Ma Rainey, the blues singer Bessie Smith had traveled with. He began taking her to out-of-town churches for concerts and her reputation began to grow almost as fast as you are.

In 1946, Mahalia's first record was released. She would go on to become the most famous gospel singer in the world, and in 1976 she received (posthumously) a Grammy Lifetime Achievement Award. Mahalia was a close friend of Martin Luther King, Jr., and at the March on Washington, he asked her to sing right before he gave his famous "I Have a Dream" speech.

Mahalia Jackson had a big voice, and she could go from a high note to a low one as easily as you put one foot in front of the other. She could hold a note until you thought she should run out of breath, and she could put together a lot of notes in a line of music that would take *your* breath away. And she did it as easily as a cloud floats across the sky.

When I was a teenager, I was attending a meeting in Chicago with my church youth group. Mahalia came to our meeting and sang a few songs. I knew who she was and I'm sorry now that I didn't have sense enough to appreciate listening to one of the greatest singers of the twentieth century. I hope you won't make the same mistake if you get a chance to hear some of the great singers of today. ◢

Born April 4, 1915, Rolling Fork, Mississippi
Died April 30, 1983, Chicago, Illinois

The way to defeat trouble is to look it straight in the eye.
That's what I was doing when I sang my blues. / MUDDY WATERS

MUDDY WATERS

His real name was McKinley Morganfield. However, when he was little, his grandmother, who raised him, noticed that he liked to play in mud puddles. She called him "my little muddy baby." Others heard the nickname and started calling him "Muddy Waters."

Music was all around him on the Stovall Plantation, where Muddy grew up, outside Clarksdale, Mississippi. He heard it in church, in the lonesome wail of field hollers, and in the train whistles crying across the flat empty darkness of the night countryside. When he was three years old he would beat on the bottoms of tin cans or buckets and try to sing. He was seven when he got his first real instrument—a harmonica.

Muddy quit school when he was ten and went to work full-time in the cotton fields, making between fifty and seventy-five cents a day. "I didn't really know that you need[ed] schooling down through the years," he said years later. He never learned to read and write, and called it one of the biggest mistakes of his life.

By age thirteen, Muddy was playing harmonica at Saturday-night fish fries. A year later he began singing and formed a band with two older men. He was

THE SOUND OF THE INSTRUMENTS IN MUDDY'S BAND MERGED INTO ONE, SO THAT NO INSTRUMENT STOOD OUT OVER ANOTHER

fortunate to grow up at a time when the people who made the blues famous were putting out records and playing in jook joints all over the Mississippi Delta: Blind Lemon Jefferson, Charlie Patton, Big Joe Williams, the Mississippi Sheiks, Willie Brown, Robert Johnson, and the legendary Son House, who taught Robert Johnson. Hearing men like these inspired Muddy to learn the guitar when he was seventeen. He would later describe his sound as "part of my own, part of Son House, and a little part of Robert Johnson."

In the early 1940s, Muddy was recorded by the folklorists John Work of Fisk University and Alan Lomax from the Library of Congress. When the recordings were played back, Muddy heard himself for the first time. Of that moment he later said, "I thought, man, this boy can sing the blues. And I was surprised because I didn't know I sang like that."

In 1943 he moved to Chicago, where he got a job driving a truck during the day and spent his nights playing at parties. He started a band, and in 1948 made his first commercial record, "I Can't Be Satisfied." The record company pressed three thousand copies to sell in Chicago only and was amazed when all of them sold in twenty-four hours.

In the early 1960s, some young English musicians with a lead singer named Mick Jagger formed a group and took their name, The Rolling Stones, from a song of Muddy's called "Rollin' Stone." Keith Richards, the group's lead guitarist, said they started the band just "to turn other people on to Muddy Waters." When another British group, the Beatles, made their first trip to the United States, in 1964, they were asked what they would like to see. They answered, "Bo Diddley [another blues singer] and Muddy Waters."

Many musicians have acknowledged being influenced by Muddy, including jazzmen John Coltrane, Dizzy Gillespie, and Cannonball Adderley; country

HOLDING EVERYTHING TOGETHER WAS

MUDDY'S VOICE

singer Carl Perkins; pop idol Elvis Presley; and rock musicians Jimi Hendrix and Eric Clapton.

I remember Muddy myself. The first time I saw him was shortly after I moved up north from Nashville, Tennessee. His band was playing in the Sculpture Garden at the Museum of Modern Art in New York in the autumn of 1961. There he stood, among the sculptures of Brancusi, Giacometti, Henry Moore, and Alexander Calder, singing the blues to an audience of white people—and me! The sun was going down, and the skyscrapers of midtown Manhattan hovered over us, but he and his band rocked like they were playing at a barbecue in somebody's yard down in Mississippi. I had never seen a black man carry himself with the confidence and dignity that Muddy Waters did. He made me feel like I could deal with anything the world put in my path. His were the blues of joy, exuberance, and triumph.

Muddy's band was composed of a piano, guitar, bass, harmonica, and drums, but their sound merged into one, so that no instrument stood out over another. Holding everything together was Muddy's voice, which could go from a growl to a falsetto in the blink of an eye.

He won six Grammys, played at the White House for President Carter, and was inducted into the Blues Foundation Hall of Fame in 1980 and posthumously into the Rock and Roll Hall of Fame in 1987, along with B.B. King and Aretha Franklin. ■

People have told me that she and I share the same sort of sadness in our voice. I don't know where that comes from—in her or in me—but it's there. The woman was a natural, always her own, strange self. / RAY CHARLES

She was living "black is beautiful" before it was fashionable. / MAE WEISS, FRIEND

Born April 7, 1915, Baltimore, Maryland
Died July 17, 1959, New York City

Lady Day. That was the name given to her by Lester Young, the great jazz saxophonist and one of her best friends. The name fit the way sparkle fits diamonds.

Billie Holiday's mother was only thirteen years old and her father was fifteen when she was born. They named her Eleanora, but because she was such a tomboy, her father called her Bill. She lengthened it to Billie to make it sound more ladylike.

Before Billie was ten she was listening to the records of Bessie Smith and Louis Armstrong, the coronet and trumpet player who was one of the fathers of jazz music. (When Billie Holiday started making records, Louis Armstrong played on some of them.) Even when she was a child, music affected her deeply. Billie said once that she could listen to a record and one day it would make her so sad she would "cry up a storm," and the next day the same record would make her very happy.

She wanted to sing like Bessie Smith, but Billie's voice was small. However, in the sound Louis Armstrong got from the coronet and trumpet, and the way in which he shaped musical phrases, she found her voice. Billie

23

She didn't just SING the words, she reached DEEP inside them UNTIL SHE COULD feel their HEARTS beating

said that between Bessie Smith and Louis Armstrong, "[I] sorta got Billie Holiday."

Except for music, her life was not happy. Although her father was a jazz musician, he took no interest in her, musically or personally. Her mother was little more than a child trying to raise a child, and she couldn't give Billie the discipline and structure a child needs. When Billie was nine years old and in the fourth grade, she played hooky from school so much the police put her in reform school, which is a prison for children. She dropped out of school for good after fifth grade.

Billie was fourteen when she moved from Baltimore to New York City, where her mother had found a job, and lived in Harlem. Billie came to Harlem at the time when a new form of music called jazz was being created by the best musicians in the world—Louis Armstrong, Benny Goodman, Teddy Wilson, and Bessie Smith, as well as the big bands of Duke Ellington, Chick Webb, and Fletcher Henderson, with whom Billie's father played for a while.

That first year in Harlem, Billie Holiday started singing professionally and was soon making records. She became known for two things: the white gardenia she always wore in her hair and a song called "Strange Fruit." Whenever she performed, this was always her last song. It was a song about the bodies of black men who had been lynched hanging from trees like pieces of fruit, strange fruit. She sang it in a small voice that sounded like loneliness as white as grief.

Billie Holiday's friends said she was truly herself only when she was singing. Music was the place where she could express her feelings, and for her, feeling was everything. Billie once said, "Without feeling, whatever you do amounts to nothing." She didn't just sing the words of the songs; she reached deep inside the words until she could feel their hearts beating. She knew that words are alive, and if you get close enough you can hear them breathe and feel them sweat and taste their tears.

I guess she put so much into music, there wasn't much left over for living. John Kirby, a bassist who played with her, said, "Her only vice was herself." She was arrested several times for using heroin, but her death was caused by a lifetime of heavy drinking.

I remember the day she died. It was the summer of 1959. I was twenty years old and was living in the section of San Francisco called North Beach. I was walking up Grant Street just past Columbus Avenue the afternoon of July 17 when a friend stopped me and said, "Lady Day died." When you can remember where you were when you heard somebody died, that person has a place in your heart.

Frank Sinatra called her "the greatest single musical influence on me" and said that in the twenty years before her death, she was "unquestionably the most important influence on American popular singing."

In 1972 a movie called "Lady Sings the Blues" came out with Diana Ross as Lady Day. Diana did a good job, but very little in the movie was true to Billie Holiday's life.

The best way to appreciate Billie Holiday is in your feelings. She once said, "There's two kinds of blues. There's happy blues and sad blues. The blues is sort of a mixed-up thing. You just have to feel it." ◢

B.B. KING

Born September 16, 1925,
Blue Lake, Mississippi

Words aren't my friends. Music is. Sounds, notes, rhythms. I talk through music. My aim is to express the longing in my soul and the joy in my heart. If I do that, I feel fulfilled. / B.B. KING

He was born Riley B. King, but the "B" didn't stand for anything. His parents divorced when he was four or five and his mother moved to a plantation outside Kilmichael, Mississippi, where he lived with her and his grandmother. He was milking twenty cows a day by age six.

B.B.'s mother and grandmother died before he was eleven. He could have lived with relatives on the plantation, but B.B. said that "from ages ten until thirteen I lived alone." His relatives probably saw to it that he was fed every day, but B.B. said he "didn't want to live with anyone except the memory of my mother and her mother."

He was thirteen when his father appeared one day and said, "You're gonna live with me now." B.B. was both excited and scared to go live with his father in the town of Lexington, Mississippi. But after six months B.B. was so unhappy, he left without telling his father and went back to the plantation. It took him two days to get there on his bicycle. But someone was living in what had been his cabin, and his relatives had moved to a plantation outside Indianola, Mississippi, so he went there.

Music was always part of B.B.'s life. He once said that the music he heard

LUCILLE,

which is what he calls his guitar, is another voice, singing in pure music what there are no words for

in church "got all over my body and made me wanna jump." The preacher of his church, Archie Fair, was a relative who gave B.B. his first guitar lessons, telling him the guitar was "another way to express God's love."

B.B. also listened to the records of Blind Lemon Jefferson, whom B.B. liked because he "put so much feeling into his words until I believed everything he sang. [He] was strong and direct and bone-close to my home." B.B. still listens to Blind Lemon's music every day.

He joined a group called the "Famous St. John Gospel Singers," but he also liked going to a club in Indianola to listen to jazz and blues. Too young to go inside, B.B. stood in the alley and looked through the slats of the building. The Count Basie Band, Charlie Parker, and bluesmen Sonny Boy Williamson and Robert Junior Lockwood, Robert Johnson's stepson, were some of the great musicians he heard there. The shows ended late at night and B.B. had to walk eight miles back to the plantation. He said he didn't mind because "I'd still hear those blues; under the glow of a white Mississippi moon, I'd sing the blues out loud, singing to the birds or the squirrels or to God above, singing because my heart was happy."

He began singing on street corners in Indianola and quickly learned that people put more money in his hat when he sang the blues than when he sang gospel. B.B. dropped out of school in the tenth grade. "The longer I live, the more I see how I shortchanged myself. I hate that I never went to college. I feel like I'm missing a component—a way of understanding the world—that only more schooling could have provided," he has lamented.

At age twenty, B.B. went to Memphis, Tennessee, and to the street there that is famous for the blues, Beale Street. When B.B. talked a radio station into giving him a daily ten-minute show, the station decided to call him Beale Street Blues Boy. He started getting mail addressed to "Blues Boy" and was soon known simply as "B.B."

In 1952, he had his first hit record, "Three O'Clock Blues," and has been recording and performing ever since. He has received more honorary degrees from colleges and universities than any other blues singer, as well as numerous music awards. These include seventeen Grammy nominations and seven Grammys, and election to the Blues Foundation Hall of Fame in 1980 and the Rock and Roll Hall of Fame in 1987, with Muddy Waters and Aretha Franklin. He won an MTV video award for a video he did with Bono and U2. He was invited to the White House by presidents Bush and Clinton, played for Queen Elizabeth and Prince Philip of England, and has a star on the Hollywood Walk of Fame.

B.B. has a home in Las Vegas, Nevada, where he keeps a collection of a million records, CDs, videotapes, and books. Even though he dropped out of school in the tenth grade, he loves to read. A funny thing about B.B., though, is that because his grandmother told him scary stories when he was a boy, he's still afraid of the dark and sleeps with a night-light on.

B.B. is the master of playing on one string of his guitar. He plays in short, piercing phrases that make you feel like something is biting at your soul. Lucille, which is what he calls his guitar, is like another voice, singing in pure music what there are no words for. When he plays, B.B. closes his eyes and scrunches up his face like he's in pain. But that's because his feelings are going straight from his heart into his fingers.

RAY CHARLES

I was born with music inside me. Like my ribs, my liver, my kidneys, my heart. Like my blood.... I release feelings inside me through my songs. I take some of my sadness, some of the heartache, and turn it out. / RAY CHARLES

Born September 23, 1930, Albany, Georgia

His given name is Ray Charles Robinson, but he dropped the Robinson so he wouldn't be confused with the great boxer Sugar Ray Robinson. But you can just call him "The Genius." Everybody will know who you're talking about.

Ray grew up in Greenville, Florida, with his mother, Aretha, and his father's first wife, Mary Jane. Some of his earliest memories were of music. A neighbor, Wylie Pitman, owned a café and had a piano. Ray was three years old and was in the café one day when Mr. Pit, as Ray called him, started playing. Ray went over to the piano and "just stared," he recalled. "It astonished and amazed me—his fingers flying, all those chords coming together, the sounds jumping at me and ringing in my ears." From that day on, music was "the only thing I was really anxious to get out of bed for. From the moment I learned that there were piano keys to be mashed, I started mashing 'em, trying to make sounds out of feelings."

When he was five, his four-year-old brother, George, was playing in a tub of water and started struggling. Ray was not strong enough to get him out. By the time Ray ran to the house and brought his mother back, George had drowned.

MUSICALLY, Ray Charles . . .

A few months later Ray started waking up in the mornings to find his eyelids stuck together as if glued. His mother bathed his eyes until they would open, but some minutes would pass before Ray could see clearly. His mother took him to the doctor, who said Ray was going blind and there was nothing anyone could do.

Ray's mother was determined that blindness was not going to prevent him from doing anything he had done before, including his household chores. Once he did a sloppy job of mopping the floor, thinking she would go easy on him because he couldn't see. She made him get on his hands and knees and do the entire floor again.

When Ray was seven his mother sent him to a school for the deaf and blind in St. Augustine, Florida. During his first year there his right eye began to hurt so badly that it had to be removed. But being blind and losing an eye didn't seem to bother Ray. He quickly learned Braille. Then, because he wanted to communicate with the deaf students, he learned sign language so they could make signs on the palms of his hands while they read his lips.

Ray's mother died when he was fifteen. He left school and moved to Jacksonville, Florida, where he lived with friends of his "other mother," Mary Jane. The friends offered to buy him a Seeing Eye dog, but he wouldn't even use a cane. Ray said he would "rather stumble a little and maybe bang my knee once or twice—just the way sighted people do."

After a year in Jacksonville he moved to Orlando and then Tampa, where he played with various bands, including a white "hillbilly" group. This was around 1946, a time when it was almost unheard of for a black person to play in a white band, especially one that played country-and-western music. Ray finally decided to leave Florida and asked a friend to look at a map and tell him the name of the city farthest away from Florida. The friend said, "Seattle, Washington." That's where Ray went. He was eighteen.

In Seattle his musical career grew rapidly. Among the musicians he met was a young man named Quincy Jones, who would become a lifelong friend. Quincy became a major force in American music, producing records for Michael Jackson, among others.

Since 1950 Ray Charles's life has been spent making music. He has had many hit records, and appeared in the movie *The Blues Brothers* in 1980. In 1986, Ray was one of the original people inducted into the Rock and Roll Hall of Fame, along with James Brown and Little Richard. He received a Grammy Lifetime Achievement Award in 1988.

Ray Charles combined the fervor and spirit of gospel music with the blues and created soul music. But he is versatile, and when he sings songs by the Beatles, country-and-western music, or even something patriotic like "America the Beautiful," he makes familiar songs sound as new as today's sunrise.

. . . combined the fervor and spirit of GOSPEL MUSIC with the BLUES and created SOUL MUSIC

Ray Charles is also a remarkable person who has never accepted blindness as a handicap. When he was still a teenager he learned to drive a car by having whoever was riding with him tell him when he was swerving too far in one direction or the other. He rode motorcycles by listening to the exhaust of the motorcycle in front of him being ridden by a friend. He has been known to pilot planes, is an excellent chess player, fixes his own plumbing, repairs his television and stereo equipment, and types seventy-five words a minute with no mistakes.

Ray Charles may be blind. But that doesn't mean he can't see into your soul. ◢

LITTLE

My music [makes] your liver quiver, your bladder spatter, your knees freeze.
And your big toes shoot right up in your boot! / LITTLE RICHARD

RICHARD

Born December 5, 1932, Macon, Georgia

In the history of rock 'n' roll there is probably no one more important than the man known as Little Richard. If not for him, there might not have been Elvis Presley, the Beatles, or Michael Jackson. If not for Little Richard, there might not even be rock and roll.

He was born Richard Wayne Penniman, the third of twelve children. He grew up loving the music he heard at church and in the street, and had his first experience singing in public with a neighborhood gospel group called the Tiny Tots.

When Richard was fourteen he left home to sing and dance in traveling shows like "Sugarfoot Sam from Alabam." These were shows like the ones Ma Rainey and Bessie Smith had starred in. When he was eighteen Richard was offered a job in Atlanta, Georgia, with a show called the Broadway Follies. An Atlanta disc jockey liked Richard's music and used his influence to get him a recording contract. Richard made two records, but they didn't sell many copies. At that time, the mid-1940s, blacks played either jazz, blues, or what was called rhythm and blues. Little Richard's music was wild and uninhibited and didn't fit into any category anybody knew about then.

When he performed, Little Richard was like a wild man

When Richard was twenty, his father was shot and killed, leaving Richard the sole supporter of his family. He moved back to Macon and got a job washing dishes at the Greyhound bus station. But at night he played music in clubs with a local band. Finally, in 1955 he recorded a song called "Tutti Frutti," and with that song a new kind of music called rock and roll was born.

To understand what happened, I have to tell you how things were when I was growing up in Nashville in the 1950s. Back then there were black radio stations that played only music by black people, and white stations that played only music by white people. It sounds kind of silly now sitting here telling you about it, but back then, that's just how things were.

Little Richard was the one who started to change all that. He was the first black musician whose records were played on white radio stations. White kids loved "Tutti Frutti" and other records of his like "Long Tall Sally," and "Good Golly, Miss Molly." Although the words in Richard's songs might not always make sense, young people didn't have a problem understanding his fast-rocking piano and high energy.

He would jump on top of the piano and start screaming and singing in his high-pitched falsetto

When he performed, Little Richard was like a wild man. He would run on stage wearing capes and suits covered with mirrors, sequins, or different-colored stones. Then he would jump on top of the piano and start screaming and singing in his high-pitched falsetto. He'd tear off some of his clothes and throw them into the audience. Little Richard told the world it was all right to let your feelings out.

Little Richard influenced much music of the 1960s. An incredible rock guitarist, the late Jimi Hendrix, played in his band for a while. The Beatles and the Rolling Stones were Little Richard's opening acts when he toured England. Reggie Dwight, the pianist with an English group named Bluesology, said that when he saw Little Richard "standing on top of the piano, all lights, sequins,

Little Richard told the world it was all right to let your feelings out

and energy, I decided there and then that I was going to be a rock 'n' roll piano player." That pianist later changed his name to Elton John.

Richard is very religious and has stopped performing several times, once for more than ten years, so he could be a preacher. In that capacity he has presided over the marriage ceremonies of Little Stephen (Bruce Springsteen's guitarist), singer Cindy Lauper, and actors Bruce Willis and Demi Moore.

Little Richard was an original inductee into the Rock and Roll Hall of Fame in 1986, along with James Brown and Ray Charles. He has a star on the Hollywood Walk of Fame and a street named for him in his hometown of Macon, Georgia. He has received a Grammy Lifetime Achievement Award, the Pioneer Award from the Rhythm and Blues Foundation, and the Award of Merit from the American Music Awards. He performed at President Clinton's inaugural ball.

Richard calls himself the "Architect, Creator, Emancipator, Inventor, King, and Originator of Rock and Roll" as well as the "Beauty Who Is Still on Duty," the "Georgia Peach," the "Human Atom Bomb," the "International Treasure," the "Living Flame," and the "Southern Child."

And you know what? He's right! ◼

JAMES BROWN

Born May 3, 1933, Barnwell, South Carolina

> **When I'm on stage, I'm trying to do one thing: bring people joy.**
> **JAMES BROWN**

The Godfather of Soul! The Hardest-Working Man in Show Business! Soul Brother Number One! Those are just some of the titles people have given James Brown.

He grew up poor and lonely. His mother left when he was four and he wouldn't see her again for twenty years. His father worked in the woods getting turpentine, which is a kind of oil, from pine trees. This meant James was left alone in an unpainted shack with no electricity or plumbing. Although he must have been very frightened sometimes, James Brown says the experience gave him "the ability to fall back on myself."

He was five when he received his first musical instrument, a harmonica. That same year his father took him to live in Augusta, Georgia, with a great-aunt. Although James continued to see his father, he never lived with him again.

His aunt's house was a place where people came to gamble and buy moonshine whiskey. Living with her wasn't much better than living in the country and being left alone.

Although James said he was better at baseball and boxing than singing, hearing gospel music at church had a big impact on him. He liked the singing and handclapping and especially the preacher, who, James said, "really had a

The crisp, percussive rhythms of James Brown's band put a smile in your heart. But instead of using just the drums and bass to play rhythms, James uses his entire band

lot of fire . . . just screaming and yelling and stomping his foot and [dropping] to his knees." A lot of what James Brown does onstage he learned from what he saw in church as a little boy.

James Brown was also influenced by the records of Louis Armstrong, Duke Ellington, Count Basie, and Louis Jordan. He learned to play organ, drums, piano, and guitar by hanging around people who played these instruments. When James was eleven, he won a talent show at a local theater. "I sang loud and strong and soulful and the people felt it," he said later.

He liked the traveling shows that came through town, particularly Silas Green from New Orleans, which, he said, "presented a complete varied program with singers, dancers, musicians, and comics. That's what I tried to do fifteen years later when I put together the James Brown Revue."

Because he was poor, James was often sent home from school because he was poorly dressed. He said he started stealing "to have some decent clothes." When he was fifteen he was caught stealing a battery from a car and sent to prison for eight to sixteen years.

While in prison he started a gospel quartet. The group was so good that prison guards would take them to sing at hospitals. James says the prison warden, Walter Matthews, "treated me like a son. Really, he's the person who raised me. Didn't nobody do it when I was at home, that's for sure."

When he was nineteen, James wrote to the parole board and asked to be released. "I know I don't have any education," he wrote, "but I can sing, and I want to get out and sing for the Lord." The parole board agreed to let him out, but said he had to have a job and that he couldn't go home to Augusta.

How could he get a job if he was still in prison? he wondered. A few days later he was loading rocks onto a truck. A man driving by noticed him and stopped his car to watch. Finally he went to the fence and asked James, "Boy, what would it take to get you out of prison?" James said all he needed was a job. The man owned a car dealership and told the warden he would give James a job. James was freed that day.

Soon after his release from prison, James formed a group called the Flames, who made their first record in 1956. Since then, James Brown has had more records in the Top Forty than any other singer.

Although he was inducted into the Rock and Roll Hall of Fame in 1986 as one of a group that included Ray Charles and Little Richard, James Brown does not consider himself a rock and roll or blues singer. In fact, he says he doesn't like the blues, even though you can hear the roots of the blues in his music.

James's music is different from anybody else's. Every musician has a sound that is uniquely his or hers. All the instruments of Muddy Waters's band blended together to sound like one instrument. B.B. King plays short, stabbing phrases on one string of his guitar and Billie Holiday paid attention to every word of a song, and sometimes even the syllables in certain words. Ray Charles is a master of melody. In James Brown's music, it's the crisp, percussive rhythms his band plays that put the smile in your heart. But instead of using just the drums and bass to play rhythms, James uses his entire band.

But to really appreciate James, you have to see him, because he does as much dancing as singing. Nobody can dance the way he does. His legs move so fast they look like a blur. James Brown puts his entire body and soul into his performances and can lose seven to ten pounds a night just because he sings and dances so hard.

James has a Grammy Lifetime Achievement Award and was in the first *Blues Brothers* movie.

There are few entertainers as popular or respected among black people as James Brown. Songs like "Say It Loud: I'm Black and I'm Proud," and "America Is My Home" deliver very clear messages. Because of his popularity, he sees himself as a spokesman for peace and racial harmony, as well as an entertainer. The love that James Brown communicates through his dancing and singing he also wants people to give to one another, and he uses music to get that message across.

ARETHA FRANKLIN

All my songs are very personal to me.
I always give everything I have to give to every song I sing.
That's the only way I know how to sing. / ARETHA FRANKLIN

Born March 25, 1942, Memphis, Tennessee

Aretha Franklin was born in Memphis, Tennessee. Her father, the Reverend C. L. Franklin, was a famous minister. Her mother, Barbara Siggers, was considered by Mahalia Jackson to be "one of the really great gospel singers."

When Aretha was two, the family moved to Detroit, Michigan. Her parents separated when Aretha was six, and her mother moved back to her hometown of Buffalo, New York, with one of Aretha's brothers. Her parents decided that the other four children would remain in Detroit with their father, who was financially better able to care for so many children. Aretha was ten when her mother died suddenly of a heart attack.

Aretha grew up in a neighborhood of future singing stars. Smokey Robinson of Smokey Robinson and the Miracles was a childhood friend; Otis Williams would become famous as one of the Temptations, and she sometimes saw a neighborhood girl named Diane Ross, whom we know today as Diana Ross.

The fourth of five children, Aretha grew up in a household filled with music. There would be music on the radio in one room, music from a record player in another, and in the third, someone would be playing the piano. Because of her father's prominence, famous musicians—jazzmen Art Tatum and Lionel Hampton; singers Arthur Prysock, Dinah Washington, and Sam Cooke; and gospel giants James Cleveland, Clara Ward, and Mahalia Jackson—often visited the Franklin home.

Aretha absorbed gospel music and the blues as naturally as you and I breathe in air. She taught herself to play piano. Listening to the singing of James Cleveland and Clara Ward inspired Aretha to sing. She was around ten when she sang her first solo in her father's church, and thereafter Aretha was a featured singer in the choir. Even when she was a child, Aretha's singing affected people. In her school, a teacher had trouble controlling her class and would send for Aretha to come play the piano and sing, knowing this would quiet the class down.

When Aretha was thirteen, she and her sisters, Carolyn and Erma, who were also fine singers, started spending the summers going around the country with their father as singers in his traveling revival show.

However, Aretha became pregnant when she was fourteen and had to drop out of school. Even though she had another child two years later, Aretha continued singing and playing the piano. She could have been a gospel singer to rival Mahalia Jackson but decided she wanted to follow the path of the great gospel singer and family friend Sam Cooke, who had made a successful career in popular music. Reverend Franklin appreciated the enormity of Aretha's musical gifts. With his blessing, Aretha left her children with her grandmother, who lived in the Franklin home, and moved to New York City when she was eighteen.

Aretha put out a number of fine albums for Columbia Records but they did not sell. Perhaps that was because the company tried to market her as a jazz singer. She could certainly sing jazz, but, dissatisfied, Aretha went to Atlantic Records in 1967, the same company for which Ray Charles was then recording.

Atlantic Records gave Aretha the chance to sing and accompany herself on the piano, and to use her sisters as backup singers. In the very first session Aretha recorded "I Never Loved a Man the Way I Love You" and "Respect," a song that became the anthem for blacks and feminists toward the end of the sixties.

Though her sisters were backup singers on her early records, Aretha later used a group called the Sweet Inspirations. One singer in that group was Cissy Houston, who would bring her daughter, Whitney, to recording sessions. Whitney Houston remembers being six or seven and "crawling up to the window [of the recording booth] to watch my mother sing. And I'd be talking to Aunt Ree [Aretha's friends call her Ree]. I had no idea then that Aretha Franklin was famous—just that I liked to hear her sing, too! I could feel her emotional delivery so clearly. It came from deep down within." And Whitney Houston says she thought, That's what I want to do.

Between February 1967 and February 1968, Aretha Franklin put out six Top Ten singles and three Top Ten albums. Five of the single records went gold—that is, they sold more than a million copies each—and two of the albums went platinum, selling more than 500,000 copies each. At that time the only other person who had sold as many records in one year was Elvis Presley. Aretha has been on the cover of *Time* magazine, won fifteen Grammys, received the Grammy Lifetime Achievement Award, and was the first woman inducted into the Rock and Roll Hall of Fame, in 1987, the same year as B.B. King and Muddy Waters. She sang at the inaugural balls of President Jimmy Carter and President Bill Clinton.

Without a doubt, Aretha Franklin is one of the greatest singers of the twentieth century, if not the greatest! It is as if the spirits of Bessie Smith *and* Mahalia Jackson live inside her. She combines blues and gospel in such a way that folks feel like shouting "Yes, Lord!" when she's singing the blues and "Oh, baby!" when she's singing gospel. But it doesn't matter what she's singing. When Aretha sings, it makes you feel glad you're alive!

And that's what the blues will do for you. Even if you're miserable, sad, and downright depressed, the blues will make you give thanks that you can breathe air and feel the sun on your face.

The blues is life, sweetheart! And don't you forget it!

BIBLIOGR

General

Davis, Francis. *The History of the Blues*. New York: Hyperion, 1995.
Murray, Albert. *Stomping the Blues*. New York: Da Capo, 1976.
Oliver, Paul. *Blues Off the Record: Thirty Years of Blues Commentary*. New York: Hippocrene, 1984.
Russell, Tony. *The Blues: From Robert Johnson to Robert Cray*. New York: Schirmer, 1997.
Santelli, Robert. *The Big Book of Blues: A Biographical Encyclopedia*. New York: Penguin, 1993.
Surge, Frank. *Singers of the Blues*. Minneapolis: Lerner, 1969.

Web Pages

Alston, David. "King of Rock and Roll." *New Bayview*, 1992. www.kolumbus.fi/timrei/lrking.htm
Pastis, Steve. "The Man Who Invented Rock 'n' Roll." *Pop Art Times*, 1996.
  www.poparttimes.com/archives/9809note.html
Ransom, Kevin. "The Great Emancipator: Little Richard Has Paid His Dues and Everyone Else's."
  The Detroit News. August 18, 1997. www.detnews.com/1997/accent/9708/18/08180048.htm

Bessie Smith

Albertson, Chris. *Bessie*. New York: Stein & Day, 1977.
Kay, Jackie. *Bessie Smith*. Bath, England: Absolute Press, 1997.
Moore, Carman. *The Story of Bessie Smith: Somebody's Angel Child*. New York: Thomas Y. Crowell, 1969.
Oliver, Paul. *Bessie Smith*. London: Cassell & Co., 1959.

Robert Johnson

Guralnick, Peter. *Searching for Robert Johnson*. New York: Plume, 1989.

Mahalia Jackson

Jackson, Mahalia, with Evan McLeod Wylie. *Movin' On Up*. New York: Hawthorn Books, 1966.
Schwerin, Jules. *Got to Tell It: Mahalia Jackson, Queen of Gospel*. New York: Oxford University Press, 1992.

Billie Holiday

Clark, Donald. *Wishing on the Moon: The Life and Times of Billie Holiday*. New York: Penguin Books, 1994.
Holiday, Billie, with William Dufty. *Lady Sings the Blues*. New York: Penguin Books, 1984.

Muddy Waters

Tooze, Sandra B. *Muddy Waters: The Mojo Man*. Toronto: ECW Press, 1997.

B.B. King

King, B.B., with David Ritz. *The Autobiography of B.B. King*. New York: Avon Books, 1996.
Shirley, David. *Every Day I Sing the Blues: The Story of B.B. King*. New York: Franklin Watts, 1995.

Ray Charles

Charles, Ray, and David Ritz. *Brother Ray: Ray Charles' Own Story: Updated Edition*. New York: Da Capo, 1992.
Lydon, Michael. *Ray Charles: Man and Music*. New York: Riverhead, 1998.

Little Richard

White, Charles. *The Life and Times of Little Richard: The Quasar of Rock*. New York: Da Capo, 1994.

James Brown

Brown, James, with Bruce Tucker. *The Godfather of Soul: James Brown*. New York: Thunder's Mouth, 1997.

Aretha Franklin

Franklin, Aretha, with David Ritz. *Aretha: From These Roots*. New York: Villard, 1999.
Bego, Mark. *Aretha Franklin: The Queen of Soul*. London: Robert Hale Ltd, 1990.

RECOMMENDED LISTENING

Bessie Smith
The Essential Bessie Smith, Columbia/Legacy 2-CD set, C2K64922

Robert Johnson
The Complete Recordings of Robert Johnson, Columbia/Legacy 2-CD set, C2K46222

Mahalia Jackson
Gospels, Spirituals & Hymns, Columbia/Legacy 2-CD set, C2K65594

Billie Holiday
Greatest Hits, Columbia/Legacy CK65757
Lady Day's 25 Greatest 1933–44, ASV Living Era BOOOOO1H23

Muddy Waters
The Complete Plantation Recordings, Chess/MCA CHD 9344
The Chess Box, Chess/MCA 3-CD set, CHD 80002

B.B. King
King of the Blues, MCA 4-CD set, BOOOOO2OMC
Live at the Regal, Chess/MCA BOOOOO2P72

Ray Charles
Ray Charles Anthology, Rhino R2 75759
Ray Charles: Genius & Soul, Rhino 5-CD set, R2 72859

Little Richard
20 Greatest Hits, Deluxe DCD 7797

James Brown
20 All Time Greatest Hits, Polydor 314 511 326-2

Aretha Franklin
30 Greatest Hits, Atlantic Records 2-CD set, 7 81668-2

*Special thanks to my editor, Andrea Davis Pinkney,
whose enthusiasm and foresight in seeing this project
through are fondly appreciated; Anne Diebel and her team
for their fine interpretation; Julius Lester for his huge heart.*
—L.C.